Ramblings
Poetry & Haiku Collection

Paul Lima

Ramblings

Poetry & Haiku Collection

Paul Lima

Ramblings
Poetry & Haiku Collection
Paul Lima
First Edition 2025
Copyright © 2025
Website: www.paullima.com
ISBN: 978-1-927710-71-5
Imprint: Independently published

Contents

Dedication

Ramblings: Poetry & Haiku Collection is dedicated to chronically ill people everywhere. Ah, what the heck... and to healthy people too.

Introduction

The poems in this book are a collection of all the poems in my first four books of poetry – *The Tree Was A Symbol of the World: A Sick Poetry Chapbook; Seasons of Stillness: A Collection of (Mostly) Sick Haiku; Ardent Illusions: A Haiku Collection;* and *Labyrinth: Peaked – Political – Philosophical – Poems.*

By way of background, I was 14 years old when I wrote my first poem. As of publishing this book in 2025, I've been writing for 56 years. Do the math and you can figure out how old I am. I only remember two lines from my first poem:

The tree was a symbol of the world
For it was a knotty tree.

Bad pun. Worse poem. But I persisted in writing, just not poetry. I switched to prose. I published a book of short stories that I wrote in my younger days: *Rebel in the Back Seat.* However, one could not make money writing short stories, so I switched to advertising copywriting, which in some ways is like writing poetry. Then I became a freelance journalist for a decade. And then, when I had a partner and a child and eventually a dog and needed to make more money, I became a corporate freelance writer. I also wrote many non-fiction books and three novels. Poetry seemed far behind me.

Fast forward to me coming down with two chronic illnesses—Multiple Sclerosis, a neurological disorder of the brain and spinal cord, and New Daily Persistent Headache, a 24/7 painful headache—that forced me to retire prematurely. Now I was not making money as a writer and could no longer write books (could not focus on writing more than short social media posts). Then I discovered AI and used it to help me write a number of non-fiction booklets. Just as I use a cane to help me walk, I used AI to help me write.

While on Facebook, I met Robert Gillett, a chronically ill person who wrote and published several books of poetry, his first being *Beneath The Tracksuit.* He decided to publish a book of poetry to raise money for a charitable cause (not yet published or I'd give you the title). He asked a number of sick folks, including me, to contribute poems to the book. I told him that I didn't write poetry but I could contribute a short prose piece. Then a few days later a poem just kind of burst (blossomed?) out of me. And then another. And another. And another... Then I discover a group on Facebook called Haiku for the Soul. I thought: Three line poetry? Why not give it a shot?

Ramblings, my fifth book of poetry, is a collection of the poems published in the first four books. But why collect them all? Is this ego gone mad? I assure you that it is not. You see, my first four books of poetry were really booklets of 30 or so pages each, They were too short to self-publish through D2D, a self-publishing platform with a wide distribution beyond Amazon, where I have published my first four books in print and Kindle formats. D2D distributes books to many online retailers and numerous libraries. So I have combined my first four books of poetry for the purpose of gaining wider distribution. Full stop.

The book is composed of poems about my illness or lack of health, my philosophy, or lack thereof, politics, or what you might call anti-Trump/Musk rants, and several other topics close to my heart.

I confess, I don't know if my work is good, bad, or ugly. I do know that I had fun writing. With all that in mind, lower your poetic expectations, and enjoy the read!

February 22, 2025

Ramblings

Poetry & Haiku Collection

The Tree Was A Symbol of the World

A *Sick* Poetry Chapbook

ZOMBIES

We do not belong
In the land of the living.
We are like Zombies.
But we will not eat you.

We do not belong
In the land of the living.
We are not contagious
But many treat us as if we are.

Friends, family, strangers
Avoid us because
We can't participate.
We can't keep up.

We do not belong
In the land of the living.

But we do not belong
In the land of the dead.

We live in a bizarre purgatory
Of sickness and ill-health.

We used to belong
In the land of the living.
And sadly, like many who are healthy,
We ignored those who did not belong.

And now we want to cry but cannot.
We want to scream but cannot.

We want to belong
But are unable to join you
Because we do not belong.

So we learn how to embrace our fate
Begrudgingly at first.
And we find our own community:
Zombies who do not belong.

*   *   *

This is it

This is it. This is my life.
Or what remains of it.
As bit by bit it becomes
Less than a crumpled paper bag.
Less than a well-used rag.
Less than the ashes of
A fire burnt out.
Less than the words
On a page that is blank.

This is it. This is my life.
Or what remains of it.
As I never run.
As I never dance.
As I never walk.
As I seldom move.
As I sit for what feels like eternity
Until I realise I can lie down.
To sleep. Perchance to die.

But until the clock winds down.
I have nothing but time to spend

And then...
That was it.
That was my life.
Nothing is all that remains.

*   *   *

Clichés Cussed

Rome wasn't built in a day.
My diagnosis wasn't done in a day either.

You reap what you sow.
I didn't do a damn thing to sow this!

Into every life a little rain must fall.
Why won't it stop pouring on my parade?

Stop and smell the roses.
In this desert of my existence?

The grass is always greener on the other side.
My grass is brown on both sides.

Every cloud has a silver lining.
Unless as black as the one over my head.

Every dog has its day.
Oh how I wish I were a dog.

You can't teach an old dog new tricks.
You can't teach a chronically ill person to get better.

When one door closes, another one opens.
Damn, this one is stuck tight!

You can't have your cake and eat it too.
You can't be chronically ill and be well too.

It's always darkest before the dawn.
It never lightens up in here.

Practice makes perfect.
No matter how much I practice, I get no better.

Every rose has its thorn.
But every thorn does not have its rose.

Actions speak louder than words.
And if you can't act, can barely move?

You can't judge a book by its cover.
You can't judge chronically ill people by their looks.

Laughter is the best medicine.
Ha. Ha. Ha... Nope, still ill.

A picture is worth a thousand words.
Picture me in five words:
*I will **never** get better.*

Time heals all wounds.
Not freaking mine it doesn't.
Not freaking mine.

*   *   *

Think

It is difficult to think straight
When you are chronically ill.
At least ill the way I am
Where just about everything hurts.

Your condition--
The pain you are felling--
Is all-consuming.
Sometimes it is all
You can think of.

Even when you try
To not think
There is little room
For thoughts about anything else.

But still you try
To think thoughts outside
What you are feeing
Even though it is
Who you've become:

A dull guy in pain.
In pain that is never dull.

*   *   *

5 Poems Collaborated on with Artificial Intelligence (AI)

I gave AI some themes and asked it to write several poems based on those themes. I told it how many lines to write for each poem. I then edited AI's work, often cutting lines and altering rhymes and working to get rid of phrases that felt a bit clichéd. Are the results perfect? Judge for yourself. (Hint: They are not. But overall, I feel that AI and I, working in collaboration, produced some decent work.)

In Shadows

In the quiet hours of morning's pale light
A weight unseen presses ever so tight.
The body betrays, though spirit stands strong
Navigating days where it all feels so wrong.

Moments of clarity, precious and few
Illuminate paths both old and new.
Within the storm, resilience blooms
A flower of strength in the face of gloom.

Through valleys of challenge and peaks of despair
My heart beats fiercely as my soul is laid bare.

*   *   *

In the Echoes of Time

Whispers of fatigue, a constant refrain
Painting the days with invisible pain.
Beneath weary bones, a spirit endures
Strength from within quietly assures.
Amidst the struggle, glimmers of grace,
A smile, a laugh, a fleeting embrace.
Through valleys of darkness, mountains of grief

A heart pulses silently with resilient belief.
In chronic battle, the soul finds its way
Embracing each dawn: promising a new day.

* * *

Heavy heart, mind fog
Shadows linger, spirits low
Hope whispers, *Be strong*.

* * *

The Light

In days of golden sun and tender breeze
Illness came and hopped me to my knees
And stole from me the joy I once embraced.
My smile fades beneath the weight I carry.
With heavy heart, my spirit grows so weary.
My dreams, once vivid, now dissolve to grey.
Yet still, within my heart, remains a light:
I have desire but dare I choose to fight?

* * *

Relentless Tide

In the shadows of my existence
I rage against
The relentless tide.
A prisoner of this pain:
Every nerve a battlefield
Every breath a war.

My head throbs with the weight
Of a thousand storms.
A ceaseless drumbeat of agony.
My teeth, my jaw, my very bones
All scream a suffering symphony.

Who shall I blame for this cruel fate?
The gods? The stars?
The very fabric of the universe?
I curse the heavens. I curse the earth.

The sun never shines.
There is only cold, unyielding rain.
A constant reminder of my torment.
A relentless downpour of despair.

In this pitiless existence
No light breaks through the night.
I rant. I rave. I scream into the void.
Should I curse God and hope to die?

I am trapped in perpetual torment
In the grip of endless pain.
Condemned to suffer
To the bitter end.
Forever and ever. Amen.

*   *   *

TV or Not

TV or not TV?
That is the question.

There are days
When the answer is:
To pass time
And get my mind off the pain
All I can do is watch TV.
Even when there is nothing
Worth watching on.

Although there are days when
I don't even have the energy
Required to do that.

On those days
I do nothing
But sit in my chair
Or lie in my bed.
The pain shooting like lightning bolts
Left to right - forward and back
Flashing and crashing and shocking
Inside my head.

On those days
Dare I say it?
I wish I were dead.

*   *   *

Can't / Can

Can't walk without cane
And even then I go slowly
Stumble and fall.
But I can write a poem
About running the 100 yarder dash
In world record time,

Can't swim the length or width
Of a swimming pool
But I can write a poem
About completing the 100 yard butterfly
In world record time.

Can't climb a ladder.
Can't vacuum the rug,
Can't put out the garbage.
Can't sip a beer. Let alone chug.
Can't do almost anything
That I used to love.

But in my poetry I can still do all that
And more. Faster than lightning. It's not a chore.

But I'm tire of sitting On my ass
all day long. Want to be doing
More than just typing.
Want to take action
As with writing I'm bored.

But I can't. So I don't.
It's all kind of bland.
Writing words on the page
About what I can't do
With no choice but to settle
For the few things I can.

* * *

Shrinking

My interest in things
Has been shrinking
The sicker I get.

The sicker I get
The harder it is to care.
To even fake interest in *stuff*
Is getting so tough.

I confess, these poems
May make me seem
Self-centered and vain.
But I think so little of myself.

I know that is a double entendre
Not of the sexual sort. As in:
- I don't often think of myself.
- I am small and insignificant.
Both are correct.

Fact is I care less and less about anything:
War- Famine - Climate Change - Pandemics –
Poverty - Human Rights Violation - Political Instability –
Pollution - Natural Disasters - Refugee Crises

Not that I don't want to care.
It's just that I can't
Because interest takes energy
And my energy is shrinking
The sicker I get.

* * *

Some I

Some are in remission.
Some are combating minor flares.
Some are dealing with trigeminal neuralgia:
Intense pain on one side of the face.
Some are dealing with throbbing pain from head to toe.
Some have optic neuritis and see black spots everywhere.
Some are dealing with urinary or bowel issues:
They piss themselves. They shit themselves.
Some have brain fog so severe
They walk into the kitchen to get a cup of coffee
And walk out looking quizzical, no cup in hand.
Some use canes to help them maintain balance.
Some rely on scooters or wheelchairs to get around.

They all are MS Warriors
Bravely, and yes sometimes barely,
Marching to battle each day.

* * *

Some II

Imagine a painful headache that lasts an hour or two.
Imagine one that last a couple of days.
Now imagine an excruciating headache that never ends.

Those with NDPH do not have to imagine
The perpetually painful headache.
They have to live with it
In and around their head.

Some have a tension headache in the forehead
The pain feeling like a tight band around the head.
Some have a tension headache at the back of the head and neck
Some have a migraine type headache in the temples.
Some have a heavy weight pressing down on the top of the skull.
Some have their headache hiding behind the ears.
Some have it hiding behind the eyes.
Some have sinus headaches.
Some have a cluster headache on one side of the head.
Some have pain that isn't localized but is all over the head.
Some pray for just one minute of relief
So they can remember life as it once was...
Some refuse to pray.

All feel oh so shitty
Every minute of every day.

*   *   *

Bonanza

Here I sit broken-hearted.
Anything I try has me thwarted.

Walk a little with my cane.
Feet on fire. Legs in pain.
I stumble and I almost fall.
Getting nowhere fast
I hit the wall.

My head aches.
It throbs like crazy.
No energy. Or am I just lazy?

Chronically ill
There is no pill
That I can take
To ease the pain
To put on the breaks
And stop this feeling
My illness makes.

When morning comes
I stay in bed
Don't want to wake.
Want to cry.
Want to scream.
Want to shout.
Want to end this
- *swear word coming* -
F*cking dream.

Should I write
Another stanza?
Can think of nothing more to say
Other than the word *bonanza*.

As I spend my time
On this extravaganza
Filled with words
About which I do not care.
With a rhyme scheme most irregular
And a rhythm that is syncopated.

Should I change my socks and underwear?

A one line stanza.
Must be important.
Or is it just me being flamboyant?

I have an illness that is chronic.
There is no tonic
No magic elixir that I can take
To release the pain
To jettison the ache.

I so wish the words that I write
Would cause the pain to bugger off
Would cause the hurt to take flight.

Should I cease my mindless rant
And search instead for inner peace?
What does it matter?
For I am madder than a Hatter.

This rhyme is getting so absurd
It's has become so bloody stupid.
All I can think of is the word *Cupid*.

Shall I end this silly nonsense?
I have the power to end these words
But not my illness: *MS* and *NDPH*.
Google them and you shall see:
Both incurable as can be.

Or shall I write another stanza?
So I can end this poem with the word
BONANZA.

Nah. That's just cheap
And not worthwhile.
Could I end it with a smile
Even though my heart is filled
With bitter bile?

Going nowhere fast I write
Until at last my name becomes
Dearly Departed.
And this poem and I
We crawl and stumble
To an end so trivial
And oh so humble.

*   *   *

Haiku

Haiku are a traditional three-line Japanese poem. Each line has a set number of syllables: first line has five; second has seven; third has five. Traditionally, haiku contain an aspect of nature. Modern haiku often, but not always, eschews the natural element. This is my take on Haiku.

* * *

Haiku tend to have
A healthy dose of nature.
Does illness suffice?

* * *

Days pass like shadows.
All tasks now monumental.
My life forever?

* * *

Stuck in spider's web:
MS & NDPH.
Rain on my parade.

* * *

Can't get out of bed
MS & NDPH.
Another day looms

* * *

Chronic illnesses:
MS & NDPH.
This blizzard is hell.

* * *

Others sicker than
MS & NDPH.
Have a hug on me.

* * *

So simple to say:
MS & NDPH.
Bloody hell f*ck sh*t.

* * *

Think I am angry?
Your damn right I am angry.
At least for today.

* * *

The sun will come out
Tomorrow. Optimistic?
Can always pretend.

* * *

What's with the Haiku?
Not like you are a poet.
Time needs to be filled.

* * *

Water is running.
A bath is long overdue.
No final line here.

* * *

Write one more Haiku
Then you can go have breakfast.
I will starve today.

* * *

So silly sometimes.
Then why is there no laughter.
Sun rises. Sun sets.

*   *   *

Remember 60s?
Hair was long; sideburns curly.
Quickly fly the days.

*   *   *

Second last Haiku.
Writing is so much fun. Not.
Blue sky. Eyes downcast.

*   *   *

So sorry about
MS & NDPH.
Forgive me my love.

*   *   *

I sit. I sleep.

I sit. I sleep.
I wake. I eat.
Then the highlight of my day:
Eliminate.

I sit. I nap.
I wake. I grab my cane
And stumble out the door for air.
Do I dare? Do I dare?
I try to walk. I fall.
A stranger passing by
Helps me to my feet.

I stumble back inside.
I sit. I sleep.
I wake and try to read.
I cannot focus on the page.
The words a blur.

I nap. I wake. I eat.
I sit. I sleep.

Tomorrow:
I shall do it all again.
Tomorrow:
Shall I do it all again?

*   *   *

NDPH & MS Nursery Rhymes

Jack be nimble.
Jack be quick.
Jack could not light,
Let alone jump over,
The candle stick.

*

Humpty Dumpy couldn't sit on the wall.
Still Humpty Dumpy had a great fall.
Trying to walk from the bedroom to the bathroom.

*

Jack and Jill couldn't
Climb up the hill.
They could barely walk
To the bottom of it.

**

Little Miss Muffet
Sat on her tuffet,
Eating her curds and whey.
Along came a spider
Who sat down beside her.
But as frightened as she was
Miss Muffet could not move away

*

Hickory dickory dock,
The MSer stared at the clock.
The clock struck one
The MSer thought

Will this night never end?
Hickory dickory dock.

*

One, two
I am unable to
Buckle my shoe

*

Ring around the rosie,
A pocketful of posies.
Husha! Husha!
We all fall down!

*   *   *

An Illness of Another Kind

Elon – Mark – Sundar - Jeff - Tim - Shou Zi.
All at Donald's inauguration.

Remember the *Alamo*.
Or in this case: Remember *Steve Jobs*.
Like him one day you will all die.
Even you dear Donald
Although I sense you think
You will live forever.

And you all shall be
Missed by so few.
For what is to miss?
Rude crude selfish inconsiderate
And oh so arrogant
Men that you are.

Too bad you don't know it.
Too bad you cannot foresee it.
Doing so would make you
Different men. Brighter men.
Simpler smarter kinder men.
More meaningful men.
Instead of what you all have become.

You eat. You sleep.
You eliminate.
Just like the rest of us.
Some of you might still have sex
Although probably medically induced.

One thing for certain
Although you don't
Seem to know it:
Just like Jobs

And the rest of us
One day you will...

No matter how many hundreds
Of billions of dollars you have.
Because money does not
Cannot buy immortality.

Are you going to bathe
In your billions like Scrooge McDuck?
Surrounded by money
Doing nothing but quack?
You sure as heck aren't
Going to take it with you
Not one freaking cent.

You act as if money is meaningful.
It is not.
You act like you can buy
And rule the world.
Perhaps you can.
But like Alexander the Great
You're still going to die,

So do something more
With your billions & billions.
Perhaps you could use
Some of you money
To clean up this mess...
Or learn how to be satisfied with far less.

Because with or without it
You still get to eat sleep eliminate
Just like the rest.

Is that asking too much of you?
Is that asking too much?

It's all wishful thinking
Fantasy and pipe dreams I guess.
It's all my hopefulness
Turning into hopelessness
As you continue live
Until the day that you die
Not matter how much
You pretend that you won't.
Not matter how much you pretend.
Forever and ever
Amen.

*   *   *

Sex at 70 with a Chronic Illness

Seriously?
You expected
A poem here?

*   *   *

A Poem That Could Be Prose

To those who are worried
Because I write a lot
About the physical
- And mental –
Effects of being chronically ill...
Allow me to say this:

I am a writer.
And they say
- Whoever *they* are -
Write what you know.
And I know chronic illness.

For 45 years
I never touched the topic.
But then for 45 years
I was not chronically ill.

I have published a book
- *Chronic: A Sick Novel* -
About four folks who live together
Each chronically ill.
Sounds like a downer
And it ends on a sad note
Doesn't all life end on a sad note?

But writing the novel
Felt so uplifting
I sometimes forgot
My characters were ill.

In my historical fiction
The Acorn Legacy
- A novel spanning 17 centuries -
Many people are well.

You can't have everybody in history be sick.

But a number of characters
Have chronic illnesses.
Both parents of the main character
Have Multiple Sclerosis
Which I have.
And one character develops
A 24/7 chronic headache
Which I have.

And poems?
I have written
Dozens of sick poems.
Poems in which people are ill.
In which they battle their illness.
In which they are defeated.
In which people ache.
In which they are in excruciating pain.
In which people are bored of being sick
But can do sweet bugger all about it.
Because that's what you can do
When chronically ill:
Sweet. Bugger. All.

So that's what I write about
Because I am a writer
Who writes what he knows.

Who wishes he didn't know illness
But who refuses to be
Overwhelmed by it all.
Overcome by it all.
Mistreated, completed, defeated by it all.

And in that way
- If only in a manner that is small -
I fight back and shout:
"I'm still writing
 Still standing tall.'

I'm still writing
Even though
Like Humpty Dumpty
I've had a great fall.

I'm still writing and
- Dare I say it -
In my sick way
I'm having a ball.

*   *   *

Thankful

Someone who read some of what
She called *negative poems*
(I call them honest)
Asked me if there was anything
For which I was thankful.

Yes, I replied
It just hasn't manifested itself poetically.
But I'll give it a try,

Had a high school friend die
At the age of 42 from testicular cancer.
Not to make lite of his death but
Thank goodness my testicles so far are fine.

Had another friend die at 50
Alone in a flat. A raging alcoholic
He was not discovered for a week.
Which makes me thankful that:
I am not alone. I am sober.
I am still alive.

My niece, rest her sweet soul,
Died from a virulent flue at 45
With two children under five.
As sad as I am about what happened to her
I am thankful something like that
Has not happened to me.

Thankful for my sisters and brother
And few friends I have
All getting older, as am I
But still in decent shape.

Thankful for my wife
Who is loving and kind
And one hell of a fabulous cook.

I am not thankful that she
Has had to endure my crap
For 25 years but I am thankful for how
She has managed to put up with it.

Thankful for our child
(Do you still call your kid *child* at age 34?)
They're bright, articulate, outgoing and fun.
Could parents ask for any more?
They have steady employment
Supplemented by screen writing gigs
Which they love.
They're in a solid relationship
With a marvelous, smart, caring partner.

Thankful for the community I found online
Especially the 100-plus members of
Feeling Sh*tty, my Facebook group
For those who, well, feel shitty.
I am sorry that they, like me, are feeling
Shitty enough to join such a group.
But I'm thankful for the fact that it is
An open, honest and supportive crew.

So for all of the above I am thankful.
But it does not distract from the fact that I am sick.

Rather, my condition, my predominant feeling,
Distracts from all for which I am thankful.

Although I'm thankful I am not sicker.
And that I can still write.
As my poems
- Good, bad or ugly –
Attest to…

I am forever thankful for that.

*   *   *

Seasons of Stillness

A Collection of (Mostly) Sick Haiku

Seasons of Stillness

Seasons of stillness
So distressed and weak am I.
Breeze non-existent.

* * *

MS*

Some in remission.
Some combating minor flares.
Some wish they were dead.

All MS Warriors
Bravely, and often barely,
Marching to battle.

* Multiple Sclerosis

* * *

NDPH*

Imagine head pain
Severe – painful - relentless
Headache never ends.

* New Daily Persistent headache

* * *

Think

Pain so consuming
It's difficult to think straight
Crooked road meanders.

* * *

Heavy heart, mind fog
Shadows linger, spirits low
Hope whispers: *Be strong*.

* * *

Zombies

We do not belong
In the land of the living.
Nor in land of dead.

We used to belong
In the land of the living.
We want to belong

Sickness is chronic
Has us in purgatory
Ignored by healthy.

We embrace our fate
And find our community:
We so-called *undead*.

* * *

Me in five wee words:
I will **_never_** *get better.*
So chronically ill.

* * *

This is it
This is now my life.
A crumpled up paper bag.
A fire burnt out.

Less than empty words
On a ripped page that is blank.
Sleep. Perchance to die.

* * *

Does time heal all wounds?
Not my freaking wounds. Not mine.
The clock hands are jammed.

* * *

Do we deserve death?
Or illness that feels much worse?
Choice. Can we make it?

* * *

Cure my ill body
I ask specialists to do.
They are impotent.

Make a miracle
It is what I ask of God
He does not reply.

Chronically ill
Forever is what I am.
Stalwart Oak toppled.

* * *

In the shadows of
Existence I rage against
The relentless tide.

Prisoner of this pain:
Every breath a fierce battle
In a losing war.

* * *

The sun never shines.
Only cold downpour of rain.
Relentless despair.

* * *

The sun never shines.
Only cold downpour of rain.
Forgot umbrella.

* * *

Feeling so shitty
Every minute - every day.
You just described me.

* * *

Can't

Can't walk without cane
Even then I go slowly
And stumble and fall.

* * *

Walk some with my cane.
Feet on fire. Legs in pain.
Getting nowhere fast

* * *

There is no pill that
I can take to ease the pain
To put on the breaks

* * *

Glued to spider's web:
MS & NDPH.
Rain on my parade.

* * *

I sleep – wake – sit – eat.
Then highlight of my dull day:
I eliminate.

* * *

Tomorrow

I try to walk. Fall.
A stranger passing by me
Helps me to my feet.

I stumble inside.
Try to read. Cannot focus.
Words a blur on page.

Tomorrow I shall
Try to do it all again.
Shall I tomorrow?

* * *

Ring around rosie,
A pocketful of posies.
Thump! We all fall down!

* * *

So sick and sleepy
That's me now every day:
Bored out of my tree.

* * *

Thought not of chronic:
Sick folks not getting better.
Then I became one.

Think of nothing else
Now that I'm labeled chronic:
Don't wear badge proudly.

* * *

Better is never
For the chronically ill
Dull sky dark and bleak.

* * *

Nature in haiku
My f*cking chronic disease.
Hard rain pelting down.

* * *

Over

Sick but not dying,
At least not dying today.
Oh joy of illness.

Maybe tomorrow
Death will take chronic from me.
Leave me completely...

...Dead and so empty
But not chronically ill.
Haiku/life over.

* * *

Have two illnesses:
MS & NDPH.
Sicker than a dog.

* * *

Perfect for haiku:
MS & NDPH.
Poetic illness.

* * *

Thinking of haiku;
Can I write another one?
Waves crash down on me.

* * *

There is a poem
It's waiting to be written.
Flowers have all died.

* * *

I'm going nowhere.
Another day passes by.
Forest is clear cut.

* * *

The bees have all gone.
No longer hear them buzzing.
Soon nothing to eat.

* * *

Going down the road
No place in particular
One step at a time

* * *

Life has cheated me.
Ha! Look around at the world.
Haven't done so bad.

* * *

Counting syllables…
In this line I need seven…
Five more and over.

* * *

Love lost in the woods.
Don't even know what that means.
Trunks – bark – branches – leaves.

* * *

Words float on feathers
Delicate airy objects
Make writing weightless

* * *

Punctuation 1

Be the first to know
What the hell is going on.
Or the last. Who cares?

Be the first to know
What the hell is going on.
Or the last who cares.
* * *

Punctuation 2

Days pass like shadows.
All tasks now monumental.
My life forever?

Days pass like shadows.
All tasks now monumental.
My life forever.

*   *   *

God is every where
I don't see him anywhere.
Beware of lightning

*   *   *

Not all my haiku
Are about my being sick.
Bored of nothing but illness.

*   *   *

You said, "My MS"
That is why you are so sick:
What an ex-friend said.

*   *   *

Faking

Some chronically ill
Have family and friends who say
You are faking it.

Like anybody
Would fake this shit for a lark
Or for sympathy.

If you think that way
You just don't freaking get it.
We have much better...

...things to do than that.
And I'd punch you in the nose
For saying such shit

If I could leave bed
And make it over to you
Without falling down.

Which would prove you wrong.
But you are such an asshole
Not worth the effort

*   *   *

Arf woof arf yap ruff.
meow-meow-meow-ow.
Pets at it again!

*   *   *

Food for the belly
Not food for my empty soul.
What I eat daily.

*   *   *

I'm writing haiku
But a poet I am not.
Can count syllables.

*   *   *

Giant Schnauzer Quinn
Plays with dog friends in High Park
Heaven new playground

*   *   *

So sorry about
MS & NDPH.
Forgive me my love.

*   *   *

Ardent Illusions

A Haiku Collection

Ardent Illusions I

Ardent illusions
Candle flames cease to flicker
Secrets in the wind.

* * *

Silent broken hearts

Silent broken heart.
Whispers of forgotten love.
Tears fall quietly.

* * *

Chronic

Chronic pain lingers.
Endless night without solace.
My cries can't be heard.

* * *

Courage

Fearless heart still beats.
Battles fought in shadows' grasp:
Courage never fades.

* * *

Guess Who*

Time. It goes slowly
As I try to carry on.
I am not laughing.

* Based on the song *Laughing* by The Guess Who

* * *

Coward's path chosen.
Fear's grip tightens around soul.
Honor left behind.

* * *

Nought

Opposition faced.
Hope fades into darkest night.
Bravely fought for nought

* * *

Shadow

Evil's shadow looms.
Whispers of deceit and lies.
Truth seeks the light.

* * *

Trump I

Who will light the way?
Beacon in the darkest times
In the face of Trump.

* * *

Ardent Illusions II

Ephemeral dreams,
Moonlight dances on still lakes
Ardent illusions.

* * *

Lost love lingers on.
Echoes of what once was pure:
Heart's aching lament.

* * *

Endurance

Condition takes toll.
Body weakened; spirit strong.
Hope endures the pain.

* * *

Frustration's tight grip.
Patience tested on the edge.
Calm before the fall.

* * *

Tainted

Health's touch is tainted.
Weary soul's strength unrestored.
Roses fade come fall.

* * *

Coward hides away.
Fear dictates each timid step
Life lived in shadows.

* * *

Against Odds

Valiant warriors
Stand upright against all odds.
Honor guides their path.

* * *

Fight

Fight for what is right.
Battles waged in shadows' grasp.
Justice finds its way.

* * *

Retreat from battle.
Strength in knowing when to yield.
Fight another day.

* * *

Ardent Illusions III

Sunset palette of
Fiery hues: bloodshot flames
Ardent illusions.

* * *

Evil whispers lies.
Deceit cloaks the hidden truth.
Darkness masks the light.

* * *

Overgrown

Strength wanes and weakens
Chronic illness wins the war
Path overgrown.

* * *

First Love I

Love lost and heart aches
Memories of tender touch
Haunt each waking dream.

* * *

Frustration builds up.
Patience wears thin each grey day.
Volcano erupts.

* * *

Sad Lie

Bravery shines bright
In the face of darkest fears.
Courage lights the way.

* * *

Sad Truth

Feebleness grips tight
Every move a losing fight.
So bleak: moonless night.

* * *

Caught in battle's grip.
Hope fades in the darkest night
Give up. Surrender.

* * *

Evil's cold embrace.
Whispers of deceit and pain.
No light breaks through dark.

* * *

Ardent Illusions IV

Autumn upon us
Petals fall like intense tears
Ardent illusions.

* * *

Faith

Goodness prevails strong
In the face of dark deceit,
Faith lights the journey.

* * *

Last Line

Chronic pain descends.
Spirit tries to remain strong
Until final line.

* * *

Frustration's tight hold.
Patience tested to the end.
Peace found in stillness.

* * *

First Love II

Lost love is sorrow
Echoes of what once was pure
Heart's deep lament cries.

* * *

Why I Write

Body so weary
Soul feels so energetic
When I write haiku.

* * *

Coward's path chosen
Fear's grip tightens on the soul.
Honor left behind.

* * *

Question

Fight for what is true.
Battles waged in shadow's grasp.
Will justice prevail?

* * *

Fighting the good fight
Strength in knowing when to yield.
You can't win them all.

* * *

Seldom Happens

Silent strength blooms.
Chronic illness can't defeat
Spirit rising high.

* * *

First Love III

Love lost aches deep.
Memories of tender touch
Visit each waking day.

* * *

My Beating Heart

Frustration building.
Patience wearing thin each day
Peace found in stillness.

* * *

Bravery shines clear
In the face of darkest fears
Courage lights the way.

* * *

Trump II

Fight for justice now
In the face of evil's might
Trump gone in four years.

* * *

Euphemism For Giving Up

Loss in battle's grasp
Hope fades in the darkest night
Strength in surrender.

* * *

Evil's cold embrace
Whispers of deceit and lies
Hope's light breaks through dark.

* * *

On Road To Nowhere

Goodness prevails pure
In the face of dark deceit
Faith guides the journey.

* * *

Silent love endures
Heartbeats merge in tender bliss
Eternal bond grows.

* * *

Ephemeral dreams
Silver moonlight whispers soft
Twilight's tender grace.

* * *

BS

Chronic pain lingers
Yet the spirit remains strong.
Hope's flame never dies.

* * *

First Love IV

Lost love's sorrow deep
Echoes of what once was pure:
Heart's lament grows.

* * *

Ardent Illusions V

Ardent illusions
Blazing meteor rips sky
Momentary hope.

* * *

Autumn leaves falling
Silent whispers in the night
Crimson memories.

* * *

Cherry blossoms bloom
Gentle breeze carries secrets
Spring's tender promise.

* * *

Clear Nights

Flickers of the stars
Are only seen on clear nights
Celestial dances.

* * *

Morning's first light dawns
And embraces mother earth
Awakening life.

* * *

Shadows of the past.
Memories linger softly.
Time's eternal dance.

* * *

Winter's icy breath
Crystalline wonders appear
Nature's frozen art.

* * *

Raindrops on the pond
Ripples dance in harmony
Nature's quiet song.

* * *

Impassible

Mountain's silent peak
Echoes of forgotten dreams:
Abandoning climb.

* * *

Good Night

Sunset's warm embrace.
Colors fade into twilight:
Day's gentle farewell.

* * *

Whispering willows.
Secrets shared in the moonlight.
Nature's quiet hush.

* * *

Ocean's gentle waves
Endless dance with the shoreline.
Eternal rhythm.

* * *

Snowflakes gently fall
Blanketing the world in white:
Winter's brisk splendor.

* * *

Neil Young

Golden fields of grain
Swaying in the autumn breeze
Harvest Moon rising.

* * *

Desert's vast expanse
Echoes of ancient secrets:
Whispers of the lost.

* * *

Morning's gentle dew
Nature awakens softly:
Day's first tender kiss.

* * *

Forest's quiet song
Leaves rustling: the wind's breath.
Nature's lullaby.

* * *

Stars in the night sky
Whispering tales of wonder
Eternal beauty.

* * *

River's gentle flow
Carving paths through ancient stone
Nature's patient hand.

* * *

Whispers in the wind
Secrets told by ancient trees
Singing quiet song.

* * *

Spring's first blossom blooms
As hope awakens with dawn.
A quick warm embrace.

* * *

Sunset's fading light
Colors melt into the night
Day's quiet farewell.

* * *

Autumn's final breath
Leaves fall in a quiet dance
Winter approaches.

* * *

Song

Ocean's endless song
Whispers from the deep abyss
Nature's voice enthralls.

* * *

Forest's hidden path
Echoes of forgotten steps
Secret way is lost.

* * *

Whispering meadows
Softly swaying in the breeze:
Nature's gentle touch.

* * *

Environmental
Photosynthetic process:
Bioluminescent

* * *

Anthropologic
Biology evolving:
Interdisciplinary

* * *

And in the End...

Environmental...
Ozone layer depleted:
Ecosystem dead.

* * *

Ketchup

Anticipation...
Banging bottom of bottle.
Burger awaits flow.

* * *

Between

Decomposition.
Interdisciplinary.
Rock and a hard place

* * *

International
Electromagnetic waves
World is on fire

* * *

MS*

People on scooters.
People sitting in wheelchairs.
People bedridden.

Me: walking with cane.
MS treats us differently.
Chronic we all are.

* Multiple Sclerosis

* * *

NDPH*

Headache is chronic.
F*cking pain unrelenting.
Nothing can be done.

24/7
There's no relief to be found
Yeah, it could be worse.

But why compare it?
It is what it is. It is.
Live with it. Or die.

We all have a choice.
I choose life and poetry.
...Relief not a choice.

* New Daily Persistent headache

* * *

About Something

Haiku don't always
have to be about something.
One flower bouquet.

Haiku don't always
have to be about something.
Window is open.

Haiku don't always
have to be about something.
Elephants: so huge,

Haiku don't always
have to be about something.
Nature is fragile.

Haiku don't always
have to be about something.
Time passes slowly.

Haiku don't always
have to be about something.
Sick or not: who cares?

Haiku don't always
have to be about something.
My feet are swollen.

Haiku don't always
have to be about something.
Sickness. Feel so blah.

Haiku don't always
have to be about something.
Want to be profound.

Haiku don't always
have to be about something.
Never will happen.

Haiku don't always
have to be about something.
My words lack beauty.

Haiku don't always
have to be about something.
Say something silly.

Haiku don't always
have to be about something.
Last line will go here.

* * *

Evolution

Change is in the wind.
Evolutionary state.
Tomorrow's surprise.

* * *

Battle

Revolutionary
Environmental justice
Is what we now need.

* * *

Ends

This life on earth ends.
Hydrothermal vents now in use.
Future under ground.

* * *

Last Breath

Photosynthesis
Evolutionary shifts;
Thin Ozone layer

* * *

Until...

I am 70.
Have come to terms that this is
The rest of my life.

May not like it but...,
Why waste time regretting what
My life has become.

Chronically ill
No recovery in site...
Still have my haiku.

When that is taken...
When I lose ability...
But until that day...

*   *   *

Crazy to write these?
Nobody will read haiku.
Do it for myself!

*   *   *

One more haiku here
before *Bored Out Of My Tree*
Haiku on next page

*   *   *

Bored out of my tree.

Bored out of my tree.
Illness will not let me be.
Sun never rises.

*

Bored out of my tree.
Writing and reading and games.
Nothing else to do.

*

Bored out of my tree.
Apples, oranges, coconuts.
Nothing left but eat.

*

Bored out of my tree.
My life becomes a cliché.
Empty horizon.

*

Bored out of my tree.
Can still write some poetry.
Three hours later...

...I used to do what?
I no longer remember
Once there was sunshine.

*

Bored out of my tree.
Perhaps I shall eat dinner.
Though I'm not hungry.

*

Bored out of my tree.
Afraid if I stop writing
Sleep. Perchance to die...

...Death. So inviting.
Nothing more I can think of.
No final line here.

*

Bored out if my tree,
Nothing to do. Watch TV.
Could life get duller?

...The rest of you watch
But could do something other.
The difference? I can't,

*

Bored out of my tree.
Life. Can take it or leave it.
Waves never ending....

...Tide comes in. Goes out.
Sitting on shore I can drown.
Hold my breath. For now.

*

Bored out of my tree.
What's everyone else up to?
Makes me so jealous.

*

Bored out of my tree.
How long can I keep writing?
If I stop... Write on.

*

Bored out of my tree.
Are you depressed about it?
Why would you think that?

*

Bored out of my tree.
Want to write perfect haiku.
Not going to happ.....

*

Bored out of my tree.
Last haiku I am writing.
Sun sets. Moon rises.

*   *   *

One More...

Write up to the end
I will write up to the end...
Fear writing last line.

*   *   *

And Another

Book asking to be
Published. This is last haiku.
Done. Hit save. *The end.*

Labyrinth

Peaked – Political – Philosophical – Poems

Can't

Things I can
No longer do
Mount like snow drifts
At end of driveway.
Shovelling them out
Is one of the things
I can no longer do.

* * *

What I think is not
So philosophical.
But then I don't think.

* * *

Cannot describe me:
Infinite number of words
Fail to resurrect.

* * *

Imagination
Is vacant, empty, and blank.
Cloudless sky so dark.

* * *

Lucky/Unlucky

I still walk
But argue with my legs about it.
I still urinate
But my penis takes it sweet time.

I still write
But novels, even a short story,
Are a thing of the past.
If not for AI, would not even
Write non-fiction books.
I guess you might say
I walk with a wooden cane
And write with an AI crutch.

Beyond that?
Don't do much more.
I sleep. I eat. Read a bit. Watch TV.
Do some social media.
Monitor my Facebook group
Felling Sh*try
With others like me
-- *my community of losers...*
Was going to type

But to me that implies
We brought this on ourselves.
We did not.

We had no choice in the matter.
It's what life chooses
For some of us.

I know
If we are lucky we age.
If really lucky, age slowly.
If unlucky we die young.

Where in the spectrum
From lucky to unlucky
Do we. the chronically ill, fit?

I don't feel so lucky
But I'm still alive.
Although there are times
Given my conditions
(yes *plural*)
Life feels like bad luck.
Or perhaps it just is
And nothing more.

In universal scheme of things
- earth, moon, sun, stars,
 milky way, universe -
I am, we are,
as close to nothing
as you can get...
And yet
Given the fact that I am
a conscious being
it's all still something to me.

And so I walk. I urinate. I write.
I do all of it poorly.
Poorly is how I exist
as I do next to nothing
and feel as if
I am accomplishing
even less.

*   *   *

Flying through the clouds
You will start to comprehend
My philosophy.

*   *   *

Showering

Try not to trip
Getting into shower.
Cower against wall
As spewing water
Is initially cold.
Sit on stool under shower
Wash all your bits
And hair.
Stand and rinse
With hand against wall
For much needed support.
Try not to trip
Getting out of shower.
Freeze and stumble
While reaching for towel.
Dry. Dress.

Slump in chair exhausted
And fall asleep.
Wake and wonder
If you can get away
With never showering again.

* * *

Liberated from
Deep thoughts philosophical
Butterflies flutter.

* * *

The cause of dying
Philosophically is
Thought termination.

* * *

Dressing

Putting on my underwear
Has become a chore.
They go on backwards as often as forwards.
And reaching down to get them over my legs
Becomes more difficult each day.

When I put on my socks
I can barely reach my feet.
Socks often get caught
On toenails that are difficult to clip.

My track pants, surprisingly,
Go on easily enough.
I haven't worn jeans or slacks
In over a decade!
Don't worry, when you die
I shall wear my nice track pants
To your funeral.

I can get my tops, pullovers of course,
Over my head.
But getting them on straight
And pulling them down right
Remains a challenge.

At last I'm dressed.
Now all I need to do
Is brush my hair and teeth.
Don't worry I don't confuse
The brushes for each chore.
But I have a wonky arm
- my right arm -
And I am right handed
So getting tasks done
Is kind of a pain.

Never the less
Morning has broken
And I am ready to start my day…
My day of nothing to do.

But ready I am
Just in case something happens
That demands my attention
So I can look at it
Mull it over
And put it off
Forever and ever. Amen.

*   *   *

Persist

Breaking haiku syllable count
To craft a meal of poetry
Shape - Style - Substance
Microwave - Crockpot - Stove
Burners are red...

Saying less with more
Saying more with less
Saying less than nothing
I'd question the meaning of life
But life is meaningless
So what's the point
If it is all pointless
All void of shape - style – substance

But still I persist
Eating dessert while stuffed
Or dying of starvation.

*   *   *

A Positive Poem

My partner is a damn good cook
Damn good
She tends the hearth and home.

Our child bright, articulate
with a great sense of humor....

Oh you meant a positive poem
About me?

Chair I sit in all day
Is comfortable.
I'm sitting in it now
With nothing more
To write.

* * *

Caught up in a rage
I cower in solitude.
Turtle tucked in shell.

* * *

Left right left right left
Rhythm is syncopated.
Dancing not marching.

* * *

My philosophy
Is a burden I carry
Until day I die.

* * *

Normally I write about my chronic illnesses: how they make me feel, and crap like that. In this book, something a bit different happened: Political poems. Okay, anti-Trump/Musk poems. Scattered throughout the book, with the first few below. So not about me and my sicknesses, although they may be about a different sort of sickness...

*   *   *

Who is president:
Donald Musk or Elon Trump?
Mythological.

*   *   *

Trump definition:
An historical skid mark.
Will bleach get him out?

*   *   *

New kind of haiku;
Donald Trump and Elon Musk
In praise of shitty.

*   *   *

What to do? Dump Trump
In every haiku I write.
Piss into the wind.

* * *

Donald: too stupid
To know how stupid he is.
Must we all suffer?

* * *

Negotiating
Ukraine and Russian peace:
Ukraine not at table.

This is Donald's plan?
If peace after book published
Will revise haiku!

* * *

More political haiku coming, but for now...

* * *

My philosophy:
Look both ways before crossing
And then run like hell.

* * *

My philosophy:
Wait your turn in line before
You climb the mountain.

* * *

Singing in the rain
of stupidity and horror
What else can you do?

* * *

How many days has
It been? Feels like forever.
And ever, amen.

* * *

Want to fuck it big
time, and then fuck it again.
Killer tornado.

* * *

Feeling lost and blue
There is nothing I can do.
Floods of raw sewage.

* * *

K

Potassium. K.
Atomic Number: 19
Alkali metal

Soft, silvery-white.
quite reactive with water.
Store under oil.

Can float on water.
Reacts vigorously and
can even catch fire.

Crucial nutrient fertilizer
for plant growth, health and yield
Also medicine:
Treats hypokalemia
Low levels in blood.

Potassium is
essential dietary
mineral found in
foods like bananas
oranges, potatoes, and greens
that are quite leafy.

Plays critical role
in nerve functions, maintaining
electrical gradients across cells
and proper function
of heart muscles.

Potassium. OK?

*   *   *

Energy so low.
Brain is all freaking muddled.
Gas gauge on empty.

*   *   *

In Flanders field where
Poppies grow beneath the cross
Is where you'll find me.

*   *   *

Disparage warriors
Is never my intention.
Sun set is crimson.

*   *   *

Beneath deep cold sea
Is philosophically
Nothing but wet muck.

*   *   *

Forrest is naked.
Not a single leaf remains.
Trump's work is complete.

* * *

Three line haiku here.
Redundant to say three line?
What am I writing?

* * *

How to write haiku. Write sentence. More if seems right. Toss in something about nature. Break sentence into three 5-7-5 syllable lines or multiples of three. If you don't have multiples of 3 or don't have syllables right, add, remove, revise. My grass is never green. Tah-dah! Haiku.

*

How to write haiku.
Write a sentence or two. More
if it seems right.

Toss in something about
nature. Break the sentences
into three approximately
5-7-5

syllable lines or
multiples of three 5-7-
5 lines. If you don't

have multiples of 3
or don't have the syllables
quite right, add, remove,

revise words until
you do. My grass is never green
Tah-dah! Haiku.

*

How to write haiku.
Write a sentence or two. More
if you think it right.

Toss in line about
nature. Break the sentences
into three lines of

approximately
5-7-5 syllables
or multiples of

three 5-7-5
lines. If you lack multiples
of 3 or don't have

the syllables right,
add, remove, revise the words
until you have it right.

Brown grass is never
green. What's this we see?
Tah-dah! A haiku.

*   *   *

Do they understand
what the rest of the world thinks?
Yes, and they don't care.

* * *

His name rhymes with dump.
What should we do with this Trump?
Wipe him. He's an ass.

* * *

Trump is man-child.
Take that back because it's an
Insult to children.

* * *

Cause? Unknown.

Plane crashes at Pearson
And flips over as it is landing.
No passengers or crew deceased
Cause unknown.

Dark Matter makes up
Significant portion of universe.
Dark Energy drives
Accelerated expansion of universe.
Scientists don't know what makes up Dark Matter
Or why Dark Energy exists/
Causes unknown.

Déjà Vu. Eerie sensation of feeling
Like you've experienced something before.
We have all had it.
Cause unknown.

Taos Hum is low-frequency sound
Heard by some residents
Only in Taos, New Mexico.
Cause unknown.

General mechanism
Of Aurora Borealis,
Splendid Northern Lights,
Is understood, but specific
Triggers and variations?
Causes unknown.
Inexplicable cattle mutilations
Have been reported forever.
Why? Causes unknown.

Mysterious Sonic Attacks
Have been reported for decades
By diplomats and government employees.
Cause unknown.

Two chronic illnesses
- Multiple Sclerosis and
New Daily Persistent Headache –
Leave me feeling
Less than down and out.
Causes? Unknown.
But look at company I keep.

*   *   *

Trump's brains are scrambled
Like two eggs in frying pan.
Let's turn the heat up.

* * *

Americans are
shocked they got what voted for.
Four more years to go.

* * *

Heart is so calloused.
Brain and spine also both scarred.
Red roses dying.

* * *

Write political
haiku about Canada:
home and native land…

We are not perfect.
That about sums it up, eh.
Beavers. Moose. And Geese.

* * *

A failed businessman.
Becomes presidential bust.
Then does it again?

* * *

There is no nature
in haiku about Donald.
Flowers all dying.

* * *

As cold as blue ice:
Each Donald proclamation
When will winter end.

* * *

Not political
Am I. But these raw haiku
Are ripped from my lips.

* * *

Wasn't there a time
When this was not at all real?
Winter now endless.

* * *

Grieving for what was.
Don't want to be so angry.
Pillow muffles screams.

* * *

Just the two of us
Caught up in a warm embrace.
Freezing out the world.

* * *

The chair is my home.
Used to walk, cycle and run.
Hard rain is falling.

* * *

My life is garbage.
Not all. But mostly feels like
Refuge washed ashore

* * *

Time moves so slowly
As if clock hands need oil.
Sun rises sun sets.

* * *

End of to do list.
Page before me is so blank.
Forest without trees.

* * *

Can still growl like
Wildcat. Defanged. Declawed.
Sound: one hand clapping.

* * *

Heal body. Heal soul.
God has his back turned on me.
Struggle on alone.

* * *

Partner amazing.
Can't imagine life without.
These words: my flowers.

* * *

Tired of writing.
Nothing more remains of life.
Oceans all drained dry.

* * *

I'm all out of words
Other than in these haiku.
Will breath soon exit?

* * *

You may not agree
That's your political right.
But your right is wrong.

* * *

So many rights are
ending under Donald Trump.
Stomping out flowers.

* * *

Canada. Mexico.
Panama. Greenland. Gaza.
Laugh in your face, Trump.

* * *

He is kidding, right?
He can't be that stupid, right?
Not kidding. He is.

* * *

The religious right
meets the political right.
Biggest sinner wins.

* * *

Donald and Elon.
Want to use pejorative
terms to describe them.

But do not know terms
Pejorative enough to
describe them fully.

* * *

What Trump doesn't know:
Millions of people working
Right now to stop him.

*   *   *

Musk buys USA.
Can't sell it to anyone.
He's stuck with the bill.

*   *   *

Humpty Dumpty sat
on wall. Empires all fall.
Trump. Musk. Egg faces.

*   *   *

Interesting times.
It's more than a f*cking curse.
Trump reality.

*   *   *

So little nature
in haiku about Donald
Goldfish in bowl drown.

* * *

All American
Presidents have some flaws. Trump
Flawless. In own mind.

* * *

One day this shall end.
If I had rocket launcher:
Finger on trigger.

* * *

Not Trump Haiku. Honest!

Anticipation
Ketchup won't flow from bottle.
Assassination.

* * *

Blank blankety blank
Blank blankety blank blank blank
Blankety blank blank.

* * *

Haiku were spilling
Out of me. Was excited.
Now glass is empty.

*   *   *

Roses are red as
I resort to clichés to
Get haiku moving.

*   *   *

Shall this be good one?
Won't know until I reach end.
Ain't gonna happen.

*   *   *

February snow
Falling like son of a bitch.
Puppy dog barking.

*   *   *

Blizzardous out there.
Shovel snow at 70.
What am I? Crazy??

*　*　*

AI book complete.
On, about, and <u>by</u> AI.
Royalties all mine.

*　*　*

President is nude.
People admire his suit.
He smirks as he waves.

*　*　*

Politics a game.
Then Trump is elected and
Game becomes too real.

*　*　*

Worst people have led.
Worst policies put in place.
Dark ages once were.

*　*　*

Trump, what do you think
about anything you do?
Problem is you don't.

* * *

Vacant space between
Ears rules America now.
Resistance futile?

* * *

Waiting for protests
against Donald's policies.
The waves are building.

* * *

Appropriate line:
Stupid is as stupid does.
Writing about Trump.

* * *

Elon and Donald.
Proof you don't have to be smart
To become these two.

*   *   *

Religious right wing.
Americans god-fearing.
But don't read bible.

*   *   *

Donald and Elon.
Politics, money raining
on most ignorant.

*   *   *

Tennis anyone?
Haven't played in 50 years.
Think those days are done.

*   *   *

Sex anybody?
Haven't sexed in many years.
Oddly, don't miss it.

*   *   *

Better things to do
Than sex or playing tennis.
Dying next on list.

* * *

How many haiku
Have I written, all without
Mentioning illness?

* * *

Next on list: a blank.
End writing haiku and I
Have nothing to do.

* * *

People in scooters.
People in wheelchairs. I walk
With a wooden cane.

Rolling and stumbling
We try hard to move forward.
Turtles on our backs.

* * *

I just want to die.
Can't think of a thing I'd miss.
Not f*ck*ng headache.

* * *

Eliminate. Sleep.
Wake. Eliminate. Eat bit
of breakfast. Tea. Toast.

Day is before me
But no surprises in store.
Every day routine.

Maybe tomorrow...
Different? Too much to hope for.
Life: one shade of grey.

* * *

Break free from haiku
Write a 300-page book?
My limit: three lines.

No plot. No chapters.
No characters in trouble.
Is brain functioning?

Have to work to write
Five seven five syllables
And make them novel.

* * *

Others have it worse.
Do not compare conditions.
Just hate all this sh*t.

* * *

This is me trying to see
If I can write a poem
That is more than a haiku.
Not that haiku are not poetry.
Not that you can write them
Without discipline.
Not that haiku are easy.

I just want to write freely
And stop counting lines
And syllables within lines.
And not think of nature:
Do I put it in or let it be?
Decision made consciously
Is not how I want to write.
I want to be an unconscious writer.
A jazz singer scatting
Improvising melodies and rhythms
Perhaps even writing poems without words...

Who I want to be:
Writer not writing haiku.
Crimson leaves falling.

* * *

Today's to do list:
Write in positive manner.
Perhaps tomorrow?

*   *   *

Dump Trump. Dump Trump. Dump
Trump. Dump Trump. Dump Trump. Dump Trump.
Dump Trump. Dump Trump. Dump.

*   *   *

Final Trump haiku:
Speaking truth about Donald.
Makes me scream. And cry.

Final Trump haiku:
Speaking truth about Donald.
Makes me laugh. And cry.

Final Trump haiku:
Speaking truth about Donald.
Makes me cry. And cry.

*   *   *

Guess this is it
Spotlight slowly wanes
As curtains are drawn
And I slowly fade away

Final act ending.
To sound of no applause.

Too late to be best I can be
Too late to be even a little better

One show is all you get
You didn't know your lines
You improvised poorly
You stumbled and stuttered
You did nothing bravely
Worse
You did it all cowardly

People say you should have
No regrets on your death bed
Screw people
I have nothing but.

Not true.
There are a few things
I do not regret
But when I think of my life overall?
When I think of my lack of accomplishments?

I will not be hypocritical
I will not take a bow.

New Poems

Since Completing First Four Books

New

This is the first
New poem
Since compiling the book,
I sure as hell hope
Others will follow…

*   *   *

Understand

Light snow falls.
I sweep it off porch.
Slightly heavier snow falls.
I sweep it off porch
Shovel front walk and parking pad.
Even heavier snow falls.
I pray tomorrow will be warmer
And it will all melt.

Blizzard rages.
I understand why older Canadians
Move south for winter

* * *

Would like to…

Jump.
I would jump.
Would so like to jump.
But elevator to roof is broken
And I am unable to climb stairs.

* * *

Nap

I just woke up
From a nap.
Quick have a pee
Get a bite to eat
Before you have to
Nap again.

* * *

Living life in general
is difficult to do.
Living life in particular
Is even harder.

* * *

Breathe

My head
Really freaking hurts.
The good news?
It only really freaking hurts
When I breathe.

* * *

Miracles

Jesus raised Lazarus from dead.
Walked on water, he did.
Healed a leper.
Caused blind to see.
Drove out demons.
Fed the multitudes with
Five loaves of bread and two fishes.
Turned water into wine
That was better than wine already
Served at wedding.
Fasted for forty days and forty nights in dessert.
And when Devil suggested
He turn stones into bread and feed himself
He passed on performing miracle
Demonstrating just how long
He could go without food.

But then while travelling to Jerusalem
He saw a fig tree filled with green leaves
But baring no fruit he could eat.
He, the man of miracles,
The man who could go
Forever without food,
Wanted a snack.

But the lowly fig tree
Was unable to provide.
So what did Jesus do?
Snap his fingers so the tree
Would brim with sweet succulent juicy figs?
You'd think so, but no.

He cursed the fig tree.
Made it wither and die.

Maybe he was having a bad day.
Happens to all of us.
But so bad that you'd curse and kill
A fig tree?
And then not raise it from the dead?

I mean, jesus christ,
What the hell were you thinking?
Some miracle that was
son of god
Some miracle indeed.

*   *   *

Chronic Lament

I can't walk 500 miles
Can barely walk around the block
I can't ride my 10-sperd bike
Gave it away to someone who could
I can't hop, skip or jump
Spend all day sitting on my rump
I can't stand in front of stove to cook
Peanut butter and banana sandwiches
My staple diet

I can't do so many things
I forget all that I can't do

I can't write another novel
Can barely post on social media
But can pick at keyboard
To write these poems.
That are read by no one
But give me something
I can do

As I watch hands of time spin round
To mark the passing of another day
Filled with things that I can't do.

*   *   *

Socializing

If not for groups
Of chronically ill folks online
I wouldn't socialize at all.

In fact I'm too tired
To edit these lines into
Right syllables count for haiku.

*   *   *

Why I Sleep A Lot

If the pain doesn't get me
The fatigue does.
The only good news?
I don't feel the pain
When I am asleep.

I go to bed early
Wake up late
And nap one hell of a lot.

*   *   *

Go for long hikes. Not.
Do not attend gatherings.
Bright lights bother me.

Have balance issues
And am a general mess.
Garden needs tending.

*   *   *

Dave Chappelle Prose Poem

Dave Chappelle is an intelligent
articulate sarcastic and satirical comedian
who has made me nod, smile and laugh.

But I don't find his LGBTQ+ humor humorous.
He seems to take LGBTQ+ sexuality personally
as if there can be no sexuality other than straight.

It's subjective, I know, but I just don't see the humor
in his take on LGBTQ+,
as if one's sexuality defined the person,
which it does not.

Is there such a thing as LGBTQ+ humor/
Of course.
Can jokes about the LGBTQ+ community be funny?
Absolutely.

*

Q: What do you call a gay cowboy?
A: Jolly Rancher

*

90% of women don't like men in pink shirts.
Ironically, 90% of men in pink shirts don't like women.

*

"There's nothing wrong with being gay. I have plenty of friends who are
going to hell." - Stephen Colbert

*

An American came up from Seattle to visit Vancouver, saw a road called Trans-Canada Highway and thought, Damn! Canada is even more progressive than I believed!

*

Q: How many trans people does it take to change a lightbulb?
A: Just one. But the light bulb must really want to be changed.

*

Q: What kind of chocolate do lesbians hate?
A: Kind that contain nuts.

*

Q:; How do lesbians settle a fight?
A: Rock – Papers – Scissors.

*

Q: What did one lesbian say to another when trying to pick her up at a bar?
A: Your face or mine?

*

You might not have laughed at any of the above jokes
and you might find Chappelle's LGBTQ+ jokes funny.
As I said, it is all subjective.
As for me?
I'm going to tune out the LGBTQ+ part of his routine.

And I'm sure Chappelle couldn't give a hoot about what I think.
But I am free to think it, and so I will.

*   *   *

Untitled

Assassination.
Not something I believe in
Mind is now grinding

Thinking otherwise
Don't want to write it out loud
Caught in a blizzard

Nature's euphemism
Distracting me from one thought:
...Would I pull trigger?

*   *   *

And in the end
the love you take
is equal to the...
cake you bake
a song by Drake
feelings you fake
a guy named Jake
the lawn your rake
life at the lake
when the earth quakes

all of that
and for goodness sake
what will it take
to stay awake:

the love you make
in the end.

About the Author

Based in Toronto, Ontario, Paul Lima (paullima.com) is retired. He worked as a writer and business-writing trainer for over 35 years. Paul is an independent, self-published author.

Books and Booklets by Paul Lima:

- *Ardent Illusions: A Haiku Collection*
- *Seasons of Stillness: A Collection of (Mostly) Sick Haiku*
- *The Tree Was A Symbol of the World: A Sick Poetry Chapbook*
- *A Minute Saved is a Minute Earned: Business Time Management*
- *Teaching and Training Adults: How to Conduct Workshops and Courses for Adults*
- *Z Z Z Z: How To Get A Good Night's Sleep*
- *Everything You Need To Know About new Daily Persistent Headaches*
- *How to Effectively Use AI to Write Your Book*
- *How to Sell Your Products on Amazon*
- *How to Buy, Train, and Feed Your Dog*
- *Understanding Multiple Sclerosis*
- *Understanding New Daily Persistent Headache*
- *The Evolution of Writing Tools*
- *How To Fast*
- *The Electronic Story Teller: A Collection of Short Stories Written by AI*
- *The Acorn Legacy: A Novel Spanning Seventeen Centuries*
- *Chronic: A Sick Novel*
- *Geri: A Post-Pandemic LGBTQ+ Novel About Something*
- *How To Write A Non-Fiction Book in 60 Days*
- *Tell Your Story: How to Write Memoirs and Autobiographies*
- *The Accidental Writer: A Memoir*
- *How to Write Winning Resumes and Cover Letters and Ace Job Interviews*
- *Everything You Need To Know About Multiple Sclerosis*
- *Everything You Wanted to Know About Freelance Writing - Find, Price, Manage Corporate Writing Assignments & Develop Article Ideas and Sell Them to Newspapers and Magazines*

- *Six-Figure Freelancer: How to Find, Price and Manage Corporate Writing Assignments*
- *Business of Freelance Writing: How to Develop Article Ideas and Sell Them to Newspapers and Magazines, Conduct Interviews and Write Article Leads*
- *The Query Letter: How to Sell Article Ideas to Newspapers and Magazines*
- *Produce, Price and Promote Your Self-Published Fiction or Non-fiction Book and eBook*
- *Harness the Business Writing Process: E-mail, Letters, Proposals, Reports, Media Releases, Web Content*
- *Harness the Email Writing Process: How to Become a More Effective and Efficient Email Writer*
- *Fundamentals of Writing: How to Write Articles, Media Releases, Case Studies, Blog Posts and Social Media Content*
- *How to Write Web Copy and Social Media Content*
- *Say it Right: How to Write Speeches and Presentations*
- *Copywriting That Works: Bright ideas to Help You Inform, Persuade, Motivate and Sell!*
- *How to Write Sales Letters and Email: Write direct response marketing material*
- *Unblock Writer's Block: How to face it, deal with it and overcome it*
- *How to Write Media Releases to Promote Your Business, Organization or Event*
- *Are You Ready For Your Interview? How to Prepare for Media Interviews*
- *The Atheist Chronicles: Why the Beliefs of Theists of Every Stripe Are So Unbelievable*
- *Rebel in the Back Seat, Hockey Night On Ossington Avenue, and other short stories*

For more information on the books, visit Amazon or paullima.com or email paulmslima@gmail.com. All books are available as paperback and Kindle books on Amazon. Many books, not all books, are available as paperback and e-pubs on many other online book stores.

www.ingramcontent.com/pod-product-compliance
Lightning Source LLC
Chambersburg PA
CBHW081147170626
46809CB00010B/3116